HURRICANES!

THE
WEATHER
CHANNEL®

HURRICANES!

by Susan Hood

SIMON SPOTLIGHT

ACKNOWLEDGMENTS
The publisher is grateful to the following individuals and
agencies for permission to reproduce their photographs and
drawings:

Back cover and right side of front cover: NASA
Left side of front cover: Ronald and Shirley Holle © 1979.
All rights reserved.
Photo insert: NASA; NOAA; Alan R. Moller; and Ronald
and Shirley Holle © 1979. All rights reserved.
Drawings by Tova Reznicek

 SIMON SPOTLIGHT

An imprint of Simon & Schuster Children's Publishing Division
1230 Avenue of the Americas
New York, New York 10020
Copyright © 1998 by The Weather Channel, Inc.
Manufactured in the United States of America
First Edition   10 9 8 7 6 5 4 3 2
Hood, Susan.
Hurricanes! / Susan Hood.
        p.   cm.
Includes index.
Summary: Provides information and safety
tips relating to hurricanes and discusses
notable examples from the past.
ISBN 0-689-82017-8
1. Hurricanes—Juvenile literature. [1. Hurricanes.]
QC944.2.H64 1998
551.55'2—dc21
98-5156 CIP
AC

CONTENTS

Hurricane Andrew:
The Big Blow

The phone call came at 3 A.M. one August morning in 1992. Robert Sheets answered. A voice on the other end said, "Bob, I'm sorry to wake you up, but we have a **hurricane**."

That was the first news Robert Sheets, head of the National Hurricane Center in Florida, had that the **tropical storm** christened Andrew had grown into a full-fledged hurricane.

Ultimately the third strongest hurricane to hit the United States in this century, Andrew started out as a mass of hot air over West Africa. Moving across the Atlantic Ocean toward the United States, the weather system gradually became a tropical storm. Up until three days before it hit southern Florida, the storm looked as if it would remain relatively weak. Unfortunately, very warm water and light winds throughout the atmosphere fed the storm. Within 48 hours, Andrew's winds increased from 50 to 140 MPH (miles per hour).

The National Hurricane Center broadcast reports on radio and TV, warning Florida residents about the possible danger, and advising people living in low-lying areas along the southeastern coast to leave their homes and seek shelter inland. Some people listened, but others didn't.

They had prepared for the storm—waited in one-hour lines at gas stations to fill up their tanks and two-hour lines at supermarkets to stock up on extra food, water, flashlights, and candles. They had nailed plywood over their windows and, in some cases, had even hooked portable TVs to car batteries in case the electricity went out.

When the hurricane slammed into southern Florida about 5 A.M. on August 24, the winds howled like sirens. Later, eyewitnesses reported seeing windows explode and chunks of metal slice through their walls. Entire families, along with their pets, huddled together in bathtubs, closets, and stairwells. Lights went out. Telephones went dead. Terrifying crashes and explosions sounded all around, but people stayed put for fear of being hit by debris. One nine-year-old girl and her parents cowered under a bed and watched helplessly as water flooded their hallway and then their bedroom. They lay half-submerged for more than six hours, struggling to keep their heads above water. In the end, this family survived. Others weren't as lucky. Thirty people died, many crushed inside their own homes.

What does a hurricane sound like?

Some say hurricanes sound like freight trains rushing by. Others are reminded of airplane engines revving up for takeoff. One three-year-old boy reportedly told his mother during a hurricane, "Make the lion stop."

Hurricane Andrew weakened two days later over the swamps of Louisiana. When residents emerged from their homes in southern Florida, they discovered their world had been turned upside down. Trees had been thrown to the ground. Roofs were gone. Entire houses, even towns, were reduced to Pick-Up-Sticks. Clothes, furniture, toys, washing machines, doors, and more littered the streets. Children's treasures—their guinea pigs, teddy bears, tree houses, video games—were simply gone. Twisted metal light posts lying on the ground became playgrounds. Inside houses everything was covered with mud.

In the days that followed, fights broke out over food and water. In the ninety-two degree temperatures, ice became precious, costing more than $20 per bag. Robbery became a big problem. Some people put signs on their houses reading, "You loot, we shoot." Where homes, stores, and restaurants had once stood, rows of tents provided by the U.S. military sprang up. The new "cities" included medical tents, day-care tents, and kitchen tents.

When all was said and done, Hurricane Andrew was the most expensive natural disaster in our nation's history. Fortunately, a relatively small number of people died thanks to the advance warning provided by weather forecasters and the precautions taken by residents.

What Andrew Did

- The Florida towns of Homestead and Florida City were destroyed.

- Out of 2,000 trailer homes in Homestead, Florida, no more than 12 were left standing. The rest were crushed like soda cans.

- Near Cutler Ridge, Florida, 35-foot-long fishing boats were ripped from their moorings and flung 700 feet onto land— that's a distance greater than two football fields!

- According to the Natural Disaster Survey Report published by the National

Hurricane Center, about 3,300 homes in Louisiana were destroyed and more than 18,000 were damaged. In Dade County, Florida, a total of 126,000 houses were destroyed or damaged and 160,000 people were left homeless.

• More than 3 million homes and businesses in Florida and more than 300,000 in Louisiana lost electricity during the worst part of the storm. Two weeks later, some 140,000 people in Miami were still waiting for service. Without electricity, not only lights, but also refrigerators, television sets, microwaves, air conditioners, bank machines, gas pumps, even doors at supermarkets wouldn't work. With all the downed power lines, it took the electric companies six months to completely repair Hurricane Andrew's damage.

- School openings were postponed by two weeks in Dade County, Florida. Ten thousand kids had no school to return to.

What Are Hurricanes?

Hurricanes are the deadliest storms on earth. Starting as simple showers and thunderstorms, they build in size and strength. When storm winds blow 74 MPH or greater, a hurricane is born.

Speed Demons

How fast are the fastest hurricane winds? No one knows for certain because at high speeds, hurricane winds destroy the instruments used to measure them. What we do know is that if hurricane winds were cars, they would get speeding tickets! The highest recorded wind topped 155 MPH—almost three times as fast as the 55 MPH speed limit posted on most U.S. highways. In the strongest hurricanes, scientists estimate that winds reach approximately 200 MPH.

Picking Up Speed

Scientists classify tropical systems according to the speed of the wind.

38 MPH and less: **Tropical depression**

39-73 MPH: Tropical storm

74 MPH and up: Hurricane

Hurricanes look like giant spinning tops. Although the winds move at high speeds, hurricanes travel across the surface of the earth at relatively low speeds—usually about 10 to 20 MPH. They can move forward in a straight line, travel in zigzags or loops, or stay in one place.

Where in the World?

Hurricanes form in areas around the world where the climate is hot. They develop most frequently in the tropics, though not right on the **equator**.

They are most frequent during the hottest seasons of the year, in late summer and early fall. In the North Atlantic the official hurricane season takes place from June to November. In the Southern Hemisphere it's the opposite—from December to June. This is because the two hemispheres experience summer at different times of the year.

A Question of Size

At the widest point, hurricanes can measure anywhere from 200 to 600 miles across. Three hundred miles (approximately the distance between New York City and Portland, Maine) is average. That means it would take about six hours to drive across the width of a hurricane.

Did You Know?

A hurricane's clouds can reach 40,000 to 50,000 feet up into the sky. That would equal the height of forty Empire State Buildings—or ninety Washington Monuments—stacked on top of one another.

Some scientists believe that a fully developed hurricane gives off the same amount of heat as a 10-megaton nuclear bomb exploding every 20 minutes.

A Monster in the Making

How do hurricanes form? Three key ingredients are required to brew these killer storms:

1. ocean water at a temperature at or above 80°F
2. air (up to 3 miles from the surface of the earth) filled with moisture
3. winds moving in the same direction and at the same speed many miles above the earth

Given these conditions, look out! A hurricane may be on the way.

What is wind?

Wind is moving air. It's caused by the uneven heating of the earth's surface by the sun. When air is warmed by the sun, it expands and rises. Cooler air rushes in to fill the space left behind.

Birth of a Hurricane

Here's what happens when a hurricane develops.

Step 1: The sun heats the ocean waters.

Step 2: As the ocean warms up, some water **evaporates**—which means that the water changes into a gas made of tiny droplets of water. This gas is called **water vapor**.

Step 3: This warm, moist air rises. Cooler air rushes in beneath, thus creating wind.

Step 4: In response to the spinning of the earth, the wind spirals in toward the storm's center. As more and more warm air rises, winds move faster and faster.

Step 5: As long as warm water and whirling winds continue to feed the storm, it keeps growing. Once the winds reach 74 MPH, a hurricane is born! The storm is accompanied by heavy rain and sometimes by thunder and lightning.

On a Scale from 1 to 5

Hurricane Camille was one of the most intense storms to hit the United States in the twentieth century. The other was the Florida Keys Hurricane of 1935. Both were rated Category 5.

What is a Category 5 hurricane? Scientists measure hurricanes on a scale from 1 to 5, according to their wind speed. Category 1 hurricanes cause the least damage. They may break off tree branches and pull down power lines. Category 5 hurricanes can completely demolish buildings and sometimes level entire towns.

Going from Bad to Worse

In the 1970s, two scientists devised the following scale to measure the intensity of hurricanes. It's called the **Saffir-Simpson scale.**

Category 1: MINIMAL DAMAGE
Winds: 74-95 MPH
Storm surge: 4-5 feet
Damage mainly to tree branches, unanchored mobile homes, power lines

Category 2: MODERATE DAMAGE
Winds: 96-110 MPH
Storm surge: 6-8 feet
Damage: Trees blown over, major damage to mobile homes, some damage to roofs

Category 3: EXTENSIVE DAMAGE
Winds: 111-130 MPH
Storm surge: 9-12 feet
Damage: Mobile homes destroyed, large trees blown over, structural damage to small buildings

Category 4: EXTREME DAMAGE
Winds: 131-155 MPH
Storm surge: 13-18 feet
Damage: Flooding six miles inland, extensive damage to roofs, windows and doors

Category 5: CATASTROPHIC DAMAGE
Winds: greater than 155 MPH
Storm surge: greater than 18 feet
Damage: Small buildings, roads, bridges destroyed

Death of a Monster

Once hurricanes hit cooler water or land, they usually weaken and die. Many die out after a day or two. Hurricane Ginger, which raged for twenty days in 1971 over the Atlantic Ocean, is the longest-lasting Atlantic hurricane on record. Hurricane John over the Pacific Ocean lasted even longer—twenty-nine days in 1994.

The Storm Hits!

Offshore hurricanes produce enormous waves, driving winds, and sheets of rain. But hurricanes cause the most damage when they come ashore by three means— wind, flooding, and **storm surge**.

Wild Winds

Hurricane winds, ranging from 74 MPH to more than 200 MPH, have incredible force. In one instance, Hurricane Andrew carried an 80-foot steel beam weighing several tons the distance of one city block. High winds are responsible for much of the damage caused to buildings and other man-made structures.

Hurricanes can also produce tornadoes, which are small, violently spinning windstorms. These are funnel-shaped and extend from the ground up to the

KID QUIZ

Q. Which does more damage, a hurricane or a tornado?

A: It depends on the situation. Tornado winds can be more violent (with speeds of more than 250 MPH), but hurricanes are bigger and last longer. Tornadoes measure up to 1 1/2 miles across. The fastest animal on land, the cheetah, could run this distance in under two minutes. Hurricanes, on the other hand, measure up to 600 miles across. It would take a cheetah at that speed more than ten hours to travel this distance! Tornadoes usually last less than an hour; hurricanes can last for days, even weeks.

clouds. Twisters travel across land, hurling large objects, such as cars and buildings. In 1967, Hurricane Beulah sent 141 tornadoes whirling across Texas.

Flooding

A typical hurricane brings 6 to 12 inches of rain in a single day. It can flood land hundreds of miles from the storm center. When Hurricane Camille hit the Mississippi River Delta in 1969, nearly half of the 256 people killed died in floods far from the coast. In 1955 Hurricane Diane did little coastline damage, but its rains flooded Pennsylvania, New York, and New England, killing 200 people and causing $300 million in damage.

The Killer Storm Surge

When hurricane winds blow, the ocean water is pushed toward shore. As a result, the ocean level can rise 10 to 20 feet higher than an average high tide. According to John Hope, hurricane specialist at the Weather Channel, each cubic yard of water (about the size of a refrigerator) weighs 1700 pounds and hits with the force of a solid object.

The storm surge is the deadliest part of a hurricane. It is blamed for nine out of every

KID QUIZ

Q. A storm surge is a giant wave. True or false?

A: False. A storm surge may be topped by waves 10 feet or higher—the height of a basketball hoop! However, a surge refers to the sea level as a whole. In the hurricane of 1900 in Galveston, Texas, one eyewitness reported that water rose four feet in four seconds! In the end, the sea rose as much as 20 feet above normal sea level—the height of a two-story building!

ten deaths caused by a hurricane. The water can smash over people, animals, buildings, and bridges and add to the flooding misery caused by heavy rainfall.

The Eye of the Hurricane

The eye of the hurricane is the center of the storm. In contrast to the roaring winds and thunderstorms around it, the eye is calm and quiet. In fact, sometimes the sun will shine and blue sky will appear. However, when the other side of the hurricane arrives, tremendous damage can occur—particularly if people are caught unawares because they believe the storm is over.

Hurricane Camille:
One of the United States' Worst Hurricanes

In August of 1969, a hurricane named Camille slammed into Mississippi, Alabama, and Louisiana, and eventually affected Virginia and West Virginia. Winds were recorded at speeds of up to 175 MPH, though some scientists suspect they reached more than 200 MPH. Unfortunately, the weather instruments were destroyed in the high speed winds. Although forecasters had expected Camille to hit the Florida Panhandle, when it became apparent that areas to the west were threatened, warnings were issued that saved many lives

The Personal Story of a Survivor

Mary Ann was one of the twenty-four people who lived in an apartment building in Pass Christian, Mississippi, who did not **evacuate** when Hurricane Camille hit in 1969. She and her friends decided not to leave their homes as they had been warned. They thought it would be fun to ride out the storm and hold a hurricane party instead.

When the storm surge hit, Mary Ann's second-floor apartment flooded within minutes. Her furniture floated up toward the ceiling. The building creaked and moaned; the windows shattered. Mary

Ann managed to grab a sofa pillow and swim out the window—just in time. Amid the roaring winds, her three-story brick apartment building collapsed behind her.

Unfortunately, her troubles weren't over. The winds and waves ripped the cushion out from under her. She grabbed other floating debris but it was quickly swept away, too. Battered by the wreckage, Mary Ann held on to anything that drifted by. Twelve hours later, she was found badly injured in a tree top, 4 1/2 miles from her home. She was taken to the hospital and thankfully, she survived. Of the other twenty-three people who stayed in the apartment house, only one other person survived.

Today Mary Ann is alive and well. She tells everyone her story hoping that the next time people are warned to leave their homes during a hurricane, they will listen.

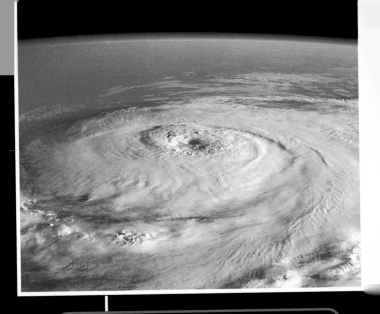

Photograph of Hurricane Elena taken on September 2, 1985, from the Space Shuttle Discovery

Satellite image of Hurricane Erin approaching the Florida Panhandle Gulf coast at 9:15 A.M. EDT on August 3, 1995

HURRICANE
INIKI

0100 UTC
9/12/92

NOAA

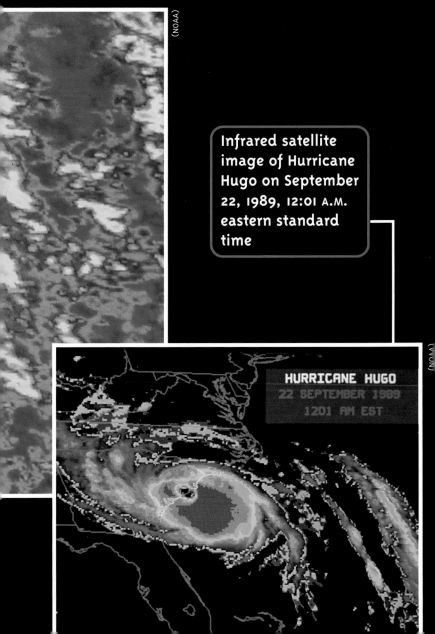

(NOAA)

Infrared satellite image of Hurricane Hugo on September 22, 1989, 12:01 A.M. eastern standard time

HURRICANE HUGO
22 SEPTEMBER 1989
1201 AM EST

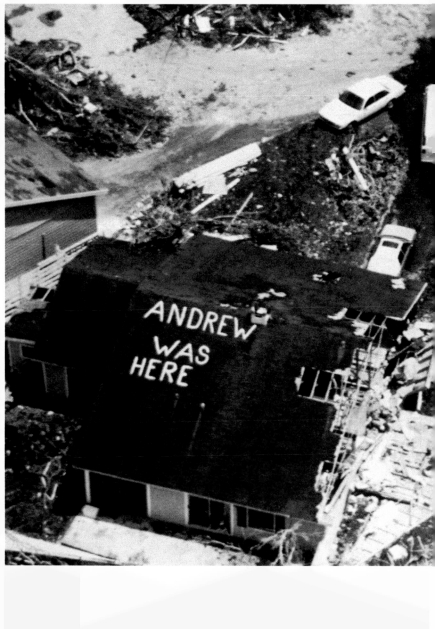

(NOAA)

(NOAA)

Satellite view of
Hurricane Andrew,
August 25, 1992

HURRICANE ANDREW
25 AUG 92 – 2231 UTC

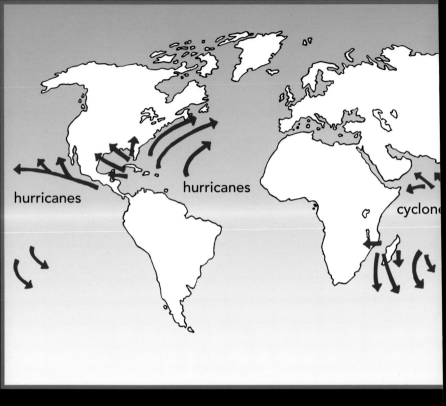

hurricanes

hurricanes

cyclone

Bird's-eye view of a hurricane

As this bird's-eye view shows, hurricanes look like spinning tops from above. Hurricane winds at the bottom of the storm hurtle around at great speeds. Warm, damp air travels upward around the eye (which remains calm), building

typhoons

cyclones

Hurricane route map

The arrows indicate the routes hurricanes, typhoons, and cyclones typically travel.

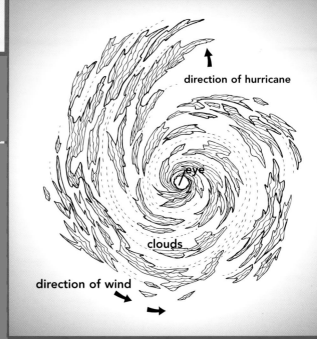

direction of hurricane

eye

clouds

direction of wind

Tropical storm over Miami Shores, Florida, on September 2, 1979

Tornado striking Pampa, Texas, in 1995

Alan R. Moller)

Worst Storm Surge Ever

Camille's storm surge was the worst ever to hit the United States. The water along the coast of Mississippi rose 24 feet higher than normal, sweeping away anything in its path—buildings, bridges, bikes, trees. At least 143 people were killed along the coast as a result of the strong winds and flooding.

Infamous North Atlantic Hurricanes of the Twentieth Century

Here are lists of the most destructive hurricanes to hit the United States mainland in the twentieth century. The first rates the storms according to the total cost of damage and the second by number of lives lost.

THE TOP FIVE COSTLIEST HURRICANES*

#1 NAME: **Andrew**
YEAR: **1992**
LOCATIONS: **Florida, Louisiana**
CATEGORY: **4**
COST: **$30.5 billion**

#2 NAME: **Hugo**
YEAR: **1989**
LOCATION: **South Carolina**
CATEGORY: **4**
COST: **$8.5 billion**

#3 NAME: **Agnes**
YEAR: **1972**
LOCATIONS: **Florida, Northeast U.S.**
CATEGORY: **1**
COST: **$7.5 billion**

#4 NAME: **Betsy**
YEAR: **1965**
LOCATION: **Florida**
CATEGORY: **3**
COST: **$7.4 billion**

#5 NAME: **Camille**
YEAR: **1969**
LOCATIONS: **Mississippi, Louisiana, Virginia**
CATEGORY: **5**
COST: **$6.1 billion**

* Costs are estimated according to dollar value at the time of the writing of the book. (Courtesy of the National Hurricane Center)

THE TOP FIVE DEADLIEST HURRICANES

Names were not given to hurricanes before 1953.

#1 YEAR: 1900
LOCATION: Galveston, Texas
CATEGORY: 4
DEATHS: 8,000+

#2 YEAR: 1928
LOCATION: Florida
CATEGORY: 4
DEATHS: 1836

#3 YEAR: 1919
LOCATIONS: Florida Keys, Texas
CATEGORY: 4
DEATHS: 600

#4 YEAR: 1938
LOCATION: New England
CATEGORY: 3
DEATHS: 600

#5 YEAR: 1935
LOCATIONS: Florida Keys
CATEGORY: 5
DEATHS: 408

(Courtesy of the National Hurricane Center)

The Hurricane Hunters

Predicting the path of a hurricane can be very difficult. As a rule, hurricanes tend to hit southern states more often than northern ones because hurricanes require warm ocean water conditions. Consequently, many New Englanders don't consider hurricanes a threat, but hurricanes can and have slammed into the northern United States.

A Deadly Surprise

In the year 1938, weather experts predicted an offshore hurricane would make landfall in Miami. When it was reported that the storm was heading out to sea, people heaved a collective sigh of relief and went back about their lives.

In fact the storm was racing north toward New England at 70 MPH. Winds were whirling well above 100 MPH.

By the afternoon of September 21, the sky had turned black and the hurricane hit Long Island full force. Rain poured and winds roared. Storm waters crashed over the shore, ripping boats from their moorings and slamming them down on the city streets. Entire houses and cottages were lifted off their foundations and then floated away. Flood waters trapped people inside their cars, offices, and shops.

Eight hours after it first hit land, the storm died out over Canada, leaving death and destruction in its wake. More than 600 people had died and 63,000 were left homeless. Crops, farm animals, and entire forests were destroyed. Fallen trees, buildings, bridges, electric and telephone poles meant that cars couldn't move, trains couldn't run, and phones didn't work.

The Hurricane of 1938 is one of the most famous of the century because of its severity and the fact that it was so unexpected. It spurred scientists to develop better ways to track hurricanes and to predict the paths they might take.

On the Right Track

Today scientists use radar, weather satellites, and computer-generated models to track a hurricane's progress. They also use information from daring pilots and their crews, who fly directly into hurricanes with weather instruments designed to measure temperature, air pressure, wind direction, and humidity. These "hurricane hunters" feed this information back to computers at the National Hurricane Center. Combined with photos from satellites and reports from ships, this information helps forecasters make the best predictions possible about the direction hurricanes are headed, when they will make landfall, and how strong they will be.

A Daring Young Man

Colonel Joseph P. Duckworth, of the United States Army Air Corps, did a daring spur-of-the-moment experiment on July 27, 1943. He became the first pilot to fly an airplane directly into a hurricane. This heroic act has since been accomplished by many other pilots because the information he brought back proved to be so invaluable. Although this kind of mission is dangerous, only one plane has been lost over the Atlantic in the last fifty years.

KID QUIZ

Q. If we have more sophisticated warning systems about hurricanes today, why is there more property damage now than in the past?

A: More damage is done because many more people live along the coastlines now than previously.

The Name Game

The English word hurricane comes from a Spanish word *huracán*, which means "great wind." People in different places call hurricanes different things. In the western Pacific, they're called typhoons. In areas near the Indian Ocean, they're called tropical cyclones. Filippinos call them *bagios*.

What's in a Name?

Today, each tropical storm that has winds 39 MPH or higher is assigned a name by the National Hurricane Center.

Meteorologists started naming hurricanes in the 1950s in order to keep better track of storms. Before then, hurricanes were assigned numbers or identified by their location. This system was confusing sometimes, especially when more than one storm developed in the same place.

"Every Little Breeze Seems to Whisper 'Louise'"

How did we begin giving hurricanes female names? According to one story, the practice began during World War II when a radio operator announced a **hurricane warning** and started singing a line from an old song, "Every little breeze seems to whisper 'Louise'". The name Louise stuck.

It wasn't until 1953 that hurricanes were routinely given female names. Each year, the first storm was given a female name starting with A. The second storm was given a female name starting with B, and so on.

In 1979 the list of names was revised to include male names. Since then, Hawaiian, French, and Spanish names have been included. Now the lists alternate male and female names. There are no names starting with the letters Q, U, X, Y, or Z because there are so few of them to choose from.

Schedule of Hurricane Names

Names for tropical storms in the North Atlantic, Caribbean, and Gulf of Mexico are rotated every six years. For example, the 1998 list will be used again in 2004. A separate list of names is used to identify storms in the Pacific Ocean.

1998	1999	2000
Alex	Arlene	Alberto
Bonnie	Bret	Beryl
Charley	Cindy	Chris
Danielle	Dennis	Debby
Earl	Emily	Ernesto
Frances	Floyd	Florence
George	Gert	Gordon
Hermine	Harvey	Helene
Ivan	Irene	Isaac
Jeanne	José	Joyce
Karl	Katrina	Keith
Lisa	Lenny	Leslie
Mitch	Maria	Michael
Nicole	Nate	Nadine
Otto	Ophelia	Oscar
Paula	Philippe	Patty
Richard	Rita	Rafael
Shary	Stan	Sandy
Tomás	Tammy	Tony
Virginia	Vince	Valerie
Walter	Wilma	Will

2001	2002	2003
Allison	Arthur	Ana
Barry	Bertha	Bill
Chantal	Cristobal	Claudette
Dean	Dolly	Danny
Erin	Edouard	Erika
Felix	Fay	Fabian
Gabriell	Gustav	Grace
Humberto	Hanna	Henri
Iris	Isidore	Isabel
Jerry	Josephine	Juan
Karen	Kyle	Kate
Lorenzo	Lili	Larry
Michelle	Marco	Mindy
Noel	Nana	Nicholas
Opal	Omar	Odette
Pablo	Paloma	Peter
Rebekah	Rene	Rose
Sebastien	Sally	Sam
Tanya	Teddy	Teresa
Van	Vicky	Victor
Wendy	Wilfred	Wanda

Never Again

Occasionally, if a storm is particularly deadly or causes a tremendous amount of damage, its name is removed from the list and not used again. This is similar to the way jersey numbers of famous baseball players are retired. There will never again be a Hurricane Andrew (1992), Bob (1991), Camille (1969), Gilbert (1988), Hugo (1989), or Joan (1988).

Watches and Warnings

Mark Twain supposedly once said, "Everyone talks about the weather, but nobody does anything about it." Although there's not much we can do to stop nasty weather, there are precautions we can take if a hurricane is headed our way.

Hurricane Watch

If forecasters issue a **hurricane watch** for

your area, it means a hurricane is possible within 36 hours. Follow these safety tips:

1. If you live on the coast or on an island, find out where the nearest shelter and evacuation routes are.

2. Make sure you have flashlights, new batteries, and a first aid kit.

3. Make sure the family car has a full tank of gas.

4. If the electricity goes off, your refrigerator and maybe even your stove will stop working. So beforehand stock up on canned goods and other foods that don't need cooking. Store extra water, and get any special medications your family needs.

5 Tie down or bring inside any loose
   items in your yard.

6 Tune in to local radio and TV stations
   for the latest weather conditions and
   advisories issued by the National
   Hurricane Center.

Hurricane Warning

If forecasters determine that the hurricane
is likely to hit within 24 hours, they will issue
a hurricane warning. Then, it is extremely
important to take these precautions.

1 Tape Xs across small windows. This
   will help prevent glass from flying in
   the strong winds.

2 Board up large windows.

3 Fill jugs and even bathtubs with extra water. You may need several days' worth of fresh drinking water.

4 Turn your refrigerator to the coldest setting. This will keep food colder longer if the electricity goes off.

5 Continue to listen to the radio and TV for storm updates. Follow the instructions of local officials. If you're told to evacuate, do so immediately! Stay calm, but don't waste time.

6 If you live in a mobile home, go to a shelter.

7 If you live in low-lying flood plains, near a river or coastline, head for higher ground. Remember, these areas can flood long before the hurricane hits and they are usually hardest hit by storm surges.

8 If you don't need to evacuate, go to the area in your house that is furthest away from the windows. Bring pets inside.

9 Beware of the **eye of the storm**. Don't go outside during the lull, because hurricane-force winds and rains can return at any moment.

Storm Aftermath

Even after the storm passes, conditions outside still may be dangerous. Be careful and be aware of hazards. Many lives can be saved if people stay calm and follow the advice of forecasters and local officials.

1 Don't touch downed power lines. They can electrocute you.

2 Watch out for dangling tree branches, broken glass, and other sharp objects in the wreckage.

3 Be on the lookout for poisonous snakes that flood waters may have driven from their homes.

4 Roads, bridges, and buildings are often in a weakened state after a hurricane and some may collapse. It's best to stay inside until local officials declare them safe.

5 Foods may spoil if the electricity is turned off. Eat canned foods to avoid food poisoning.

What Good Are Hurricanes?

No one would wish for a hurricane. They cause too much suffering and damage. And yet, hurricanes do have positive effects on the earth's weather. They are nature's way of bringing much-needed rain to drier parts of the world. Japan, for example, gets a quarter of its rain from typhoons. Hurricanes also help move warm air from the equator to cooler parts of the world.

One of most positive aftereffects of a hurricane, or any natural disaster, is the way relief efforts boost community spirit and bring people of all ages, races, and religions together. After Hurricane Andrew, churches, charities, and concerned citizens across the country responded with an incredible outpouring of groceries, clothing, baby food, diapers, money, towels, bed linens, and other everyday supplies. School children, including pre-schoolers, recycled soda cans, sent favorite books and toys, and emptied their piggy banks to send cash to those in need. World-famous singers and comedians organized their own relief efforts by donating money from concerts. Businesses distributed free medical supplies, construction materials, and advice to those whose lives were devastated.

Zoo News

In 1992, among the victims of Hurricane Andrew were the animals in a zoo called

Metrozoo in Miami, Florida. During the storm, roofs flew off buildings and fences blew down, freeing a herd of antelope, hundreds of birds, and several 500-pound tortoises, among other animals. Luckily, the dangerous animals—lions, tigers, and bears—remained inside their concrete houses behind steel bars, where they safely weathered the storm.

The koalas weren't so lucky. Three of them lost their food supply and then their air-conditioned home. Without food and unaccustomed to the high heat and humidity of Florida weather, the koalas might have died had it not been for the generosity of a private pilot. He had a runway cleared near the zoo, loaded the koalas onto his small plane, and flew them to the closest zoo with a suitable habitat. More than one hundred other people put aside their own hurricane headaches and heartbreaks to help save the helpless animals roaming the wreckage. During their work, they discovered a healthy baby antelope that had been born during the storm. He was immediately christened Andrew.

As one survivor put it, "Hurricane Andrew put things in perspective." It made thousands of people in Florida, Louisiana, and across the country grateful for the things too many of us take for granted—food, water, shelter, and family.

GLOSSARY

EQUATOR—An imaginary line around the middle of the Earth. The Earth is hottest at the equator because that's where the sun's rays strike most directly.

EVACUATE—To leave your home to seek shelter from the storm.

EVAPORATION—Occurs when liquid water heats up and changes into an invisible gas called water vapor.

EYE OF THE STORM—The calm center of a hurricane.

HURRICANE—A storm from the tropics that begins at sea with winds of 74 MPH and greater.

HURRICANE WATCH—An advisory that a hurricane might hit within 36 hours.

HURRICANE WARNING—A warning that a hurricane is expected to hit within 24 hours.

SAFFIR-SIMPSON SCALE—A scale scientists use to measure the intensity of hurricanes.

STORM SURGE—A rise in sea level caused by hurricanes.

TROPICAL DEPRESSION—A weather system from the tropics with winds of 38 MPH and less.

TROPICAL STORM—A storm from the tropics with winds from 39 to 74 MPH.

WATER VAPOR—Water in the form of an invisible gas.

INDEX